Walt Disney's
STORY OF
101 DALMATIANS

gb **GOLDEN PRESS**
Western Publishing Company, Inc.
Racine, Wisconsin

1976 Printing
Special Goldencraft ® Edition

Lucky Puppy lived with his father, Pongo, and his
mother, Perdita, and with all his sisters and brothers.
The people who belonged to them were Roger and Anita
and Nanny Cook. (That's Nanny Cook in the doorway above.)

1

Here are Penny and Lenny and Salter and Pepper,
Jolly and Rolly and Patch and Latch.

Here are Spot and Dot and Blob and Blot and Blackie
and Whitey and—where's Lucky?

Here's Lucky, in front of the television, watching his favorite, Thunderbolt.

Whenever Penny and Lenny
wanted to dig holes,

or Salter and Pepper wanted to chew bones,

5

or Patch and Latch
wanted to chase tails,

or Jolly and Rolly wanted to jump at Nanny Cook's apron string

6

or Spot and Dot wanted
to play hide and seek,

or Blob and Blot wanted to growl at the mirror,

or Blackie and Whitey wanted to take a nap,

Lucky never wanted to. He just wanted to sit in front of the television watching his favorite, Thunderbolt.

Or he practiced television tricks. "I'm going to be a television
star myself," said Lucky Pup.

Well, all the other puppies learned puppy tricks. Soon they could sit up and roll over.

They could dance and
shake hands.

They could jump
for a treat and
walk politely at heel.
But not Lucky.

He was too busy dreaming of being a television star.

One day he decided he was ready to be in a television show. So he slipped out of the house and he ran down the street. He ran around a corner. And there he stopped.

He was lost.
He did not know his way
to the television place.
And he did not know
his way home.

Poor Lucky.
He walked and walked and walked.
He tried to show people
his television tricks.
But they did not understand.
"He doesn't seem to know
any puppy tricks,"
was all the people said.

16

Finally a policeman came along. He looked at Lucky's
license tag. And he took Lucky home.

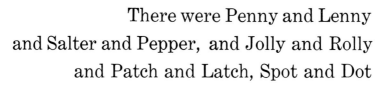

There were Penny and Lenny
and Salter and Pepper, and Jolly and Rolly
and Patch and Latch, Spot and Dot

and Blob and Blot and Blackie and Whitey,
all doing puppy tricks for treats.
But not Lucky.

19

Lucky was all tired out. He crept straight into his
basket and he went straight to sleep.

He even slept through the Thunderbolt Show which the other puppies watched.

But next morning Lucky was up first of all. "Time
enough for television later," he said. "Now I am going
to learn my puppy tricks."

And he did!